Best Wishes!

Denise Mullenoy

THE ADVENTURES OF MINKY AND BEE

Mermaid Mission:

A Shell For Nell

By Denise Mullenary

Illustrated By T. J. Morales

Copyright © 2020 By Denise Mullenary

All rights reserved

Mullenary Books - Lompoc, CA

ISBN: 978-1-0878-8443-1

To my Sister Natalie,

May this Book spark joy and bring fond memories of you and I, the original Minky and

Bee. I loved all the adventures we embarked on in the past, and look forward to what

our future holds. You are, and always will be, the Bee to my Minky, the Laura to my

Mary, and the Neo to my Cleo. You are forever my inspiration and biggest supporter. You

watch...and I see you. Thank you for everything you mean to me in my life, I appreciate

you more than words can express. For all the years we were Mermaids in the bathtub

and hotel pools, I dedicate this to you, my favorite Mermaid.

"Would you like more water?"

Early one morning, on a bright summer day,

Minky and Bee went to the meadow to play.

They crawled through the hole in the magic oak tree,

and wondered what this days adventure would be.

Once they crawl through the hole,

their dreams become real;

all missions and quests are a great big ordeal.

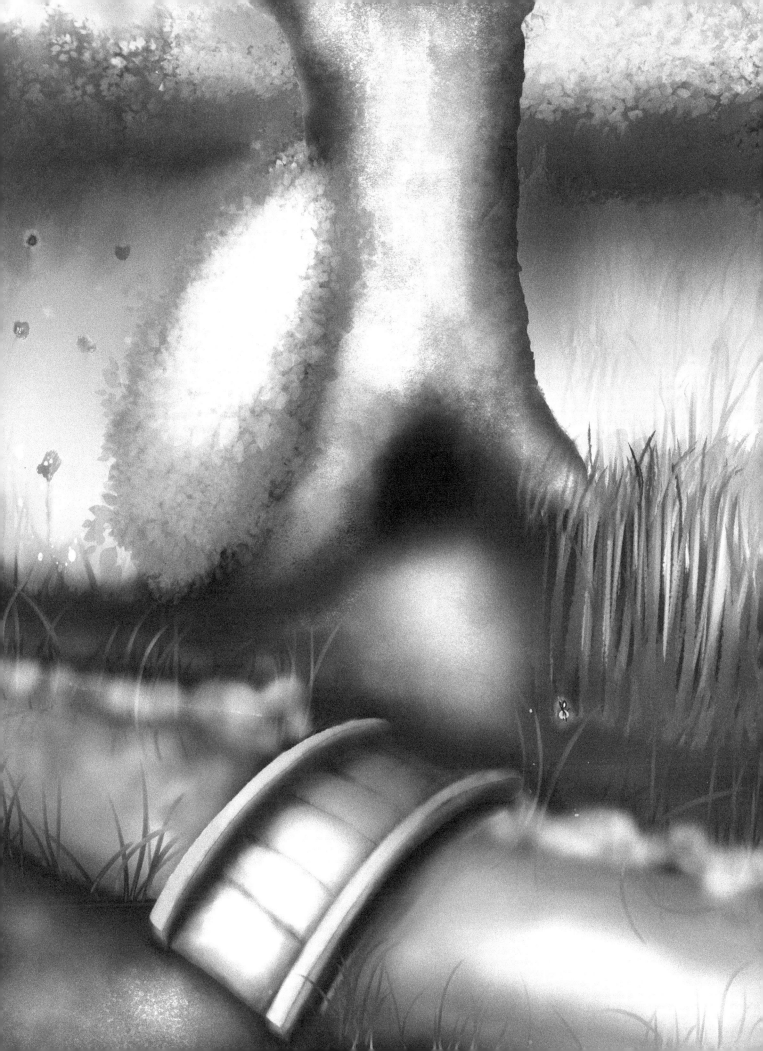

They have their old faithful friends with them there;
Miss Scarlett the fox and big Bubba the bear.

Off in the distance they hear someone cry,
so they follow the sound to find and ask why.

They come to a beach where a river runs through, and see a fine mermaid who looks rather blue.

"what's wrong?"   asks. "Dry your eyes, who are you? Please tell us what's wrong and we'll see what to do!"

"My name is Nellie, some friends call me Nell.
I'm crying because I've lost my new shell.
This shell is so special, it's magic, you see;
it was given by someone that's so dear to me.
My father's a soldier for the MerKing;
their troops went far off to help with something.
I miss him so much when he is not here,
he asked me to   stay strong and
not shed a tear."

"Before leaving he filled a shell with his voice.

When I hear him it makes my whole soul rejoice!

The shell holds his message of love and goodwill;

I listen whenever I'm missing him still.

Somehow I've misplaced it, I'm so sad to say;

I've been searching everywhere for it today."

"We'll help you!" cries Bee, "Dry your eyes, have no fear! We will look for shell, it has to be near!"

"Of course!" says, "We would all love to help!
Let us come with you to search through the kelp.
Bubba and Scarlett will stay up on land,
to look behind rocks and dig through the sand.
This way they stay dry and won't ruin their fur;
with all of us helping we'll find it for sure!"

"Oh, thank you," sniffs Nell. "How incredibly sweet.
To swim faster let's just get rid of those feet."

She reaches down to her magnificent tail,
and plucks for each girl a bright shimmering scale.

"Hold these magical scales close to your heart,
then repeat after me, I'll give you a start."

"Mermaids, oh mermaids, who live in the sea...
Mermaids, oh mermaids, we so wish to be!"

Upon this chant leaving the lips of the girls,

they flew off the seashore with sparkles and twirls!

The magic surrounded them up to their bows,

and fins now replaced where there used to be toes.

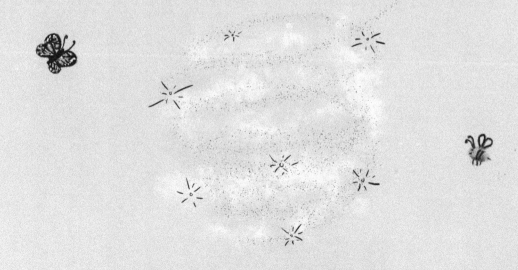

They gaze at their tales with wonder and glee,

then splash in the water, so wild and free.

Nellie giggled and watched, delighted for them,

but soon she spoke up with a cough, and "ahem!"

"Being a mermaid is wonderful, no?

We must not forget what our mission is though."

"You're right!" Minky says, "let's set off on our quest!
Not a moment to lose or a minute to rest."

The mermaids bid Scarlett and Bubba farewell,

then dive in the water to look for the shell.

Under the surface it all becomes clear;

an entire Kingdom is thriving down here!

Hundreds of silly fish dancing in schools,

Mermen and Maidens with crowns full of jewels.

A castle so grand with its walls made of pearls,

the current sways seaweed in fanciful swirls.

and Bee follow close behind Nellie,

she points as they pass by a cluster of jellies.

Their search for the shell begins at the ground;

they look back and forth and around and around.

They look behind coral that's bright and ornate,

and under sand dollars as big as a plate.

They swim to the castle to roam through the halls,

and look amongst statues and portraits on walls.

Scarlett and Bubba remain up on shore,
searching for shells, though their luck has been poor.
They sift through sand and throw rocks in a pile,
they walk down the beach for at least half a mile.

Now as their spirits begin to feel dreary,
Scarlett slumps down with a sigh full of weary.

Just up ahead Bubba finds a tree stump,
he plops down upon it and makes a loud THUMP!

with his chin on his fist he scratches his head.

What's this, by his foot? It's a glimpse of red!

He bends down and lifts the thing stuck in the sand,
and looks at it close in the palm of his hand.
A beautiful shell with a little red jewel,
to think this was not it, he must be a fool.

"I've found it! I've found it! I've found it!" He said.

Scarlett prays quickly that he's not mislead.

They take turns examining their lucky find,

then laugh, dance, and hug, and become intertwined.

Soon artsy Miss Scarlett the fox has a thought,
"Let's put it on a string she can tie with a knot!"

She digs through her satchel and pulls out some tools,
like scissors and beads, and bright colored yarn spools.

She sets to work crafting while Bubba watches,
and lays out her patterns and color swatches.

Below in the water the mermaids are sad;
they can't find the shell with the voice from her dad.

They decide to go up and call it a day.

They'll find it tomorrow they hope and they pray.

While [Mindy] takes one last glance all around her,

Bee waves goodbye to a bright yellow flounder.

They swim towards the surface by swishing their tails,

right past a mama with two baby whales.

Nell sits on a rock and the girls now have feet;

Miss Scarlett runs up without missing a beat.

Her face beams with pride as she holds up for them,

a beautiful necklace with coloful gems.

They gasp as they see what lies in the center.
Why, it's Nellie's shell in all it's splendor!

They squeal with delight as they let out a cheer,

then watch as Nell holds the shell up to her ear.

From the shell comes the smooth voice of her father;

the message he left for his beautiful daughter.

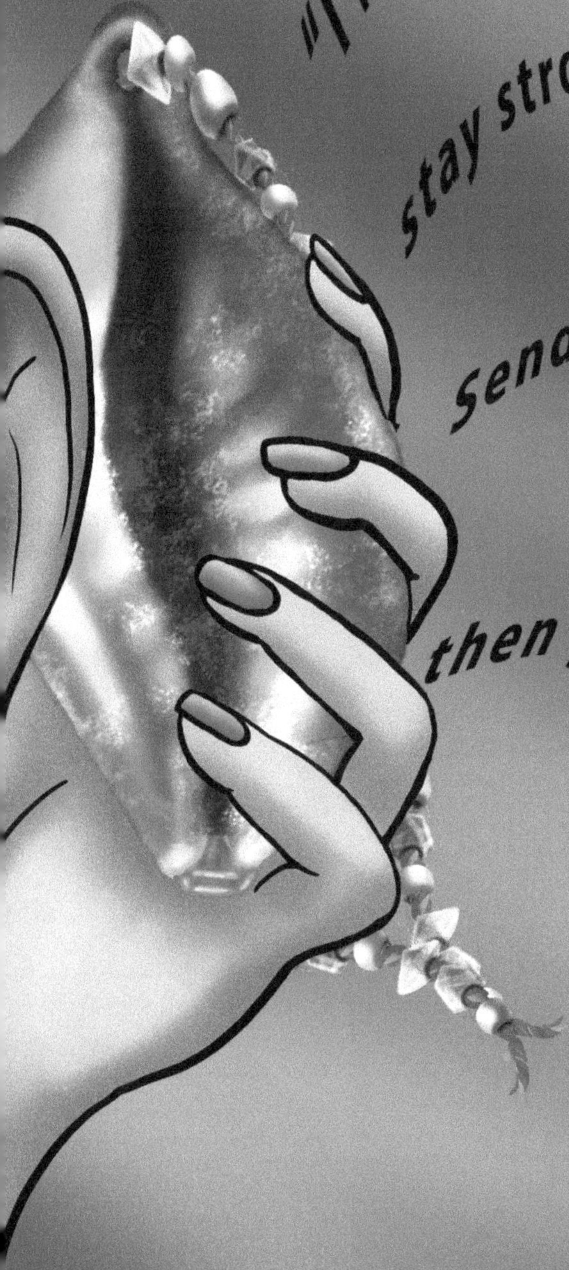

"I'm off to protect our great Castle of Pearl,
stay strong and remember me, my little girl.
Send prayers up to heaven for my safe return,
then go on with your day and don't have concern."

Nell smiles and wears her shell necklace with pride;
they sigh in relief that her tears have now dried.

Now Scarlett and Bubba and Minky and Bee,

all hug their new friend that they

 met through the tree.

They promise to come back and see her again,

to have more adventures with her now and then.

They crawl through the hole and walk home hand in hand,
to tell Mom and Dad of their day in the sand.

Do you want to be artsy like Miss Scarlett? Ask your mom and dad to copy and print this image so you can color it in and add decorations!

Look and Find

About the Author Denise Mullenary

Denise is a happily married mother of four children. She enjoys reading, writing, and a good cup of coffee!

The book characters, Scarlett, Bubba, Minky, and Bee each represent one of her own kids and their unique personalities.

Stay tuned for the next book in the Minky and Bee Adventure series, The Merry Meadow, available for purchase holiday season 2020.

Denise Mullenary can be contacted at mullenarybooks@gmail.com and followed on social media for updates on book release and signings.

Facebook: Denise Mullenary Author

Instagram: @AuthorDeniseMullenary

About the Illustrator Thomas J. Morales

Thomas J. Morales lives in a small town on the central coast of California with his dog, Bubbie. He loves his big family and as a Christian he draws inspiration from his faith.

He started his career taking art courses at Allan Hancock College and building his skills and knowledge of multiple art mediums.

Instagram @tjmorales09

CPSIA information can be obtained
at www.ICGtesting.com
Printed in the USA
LVHW071151081221
703908LV00010B/8

9 781087 884431